TWO BROWN OWLS PROSE

JAQI LOYE-BROWN
DIANA BROWN

MT Ink

MT Ink

MT-Ink.co.uk

First published by MT Ink in 2023

ISBN: 978-1-8383883-3-1

Cover design: Jaxetta.com

Dedication

To my dad, Eithel Brown for such positive vibes, and to my mum (DB)

To Tina Turner...and to the voiceless (JLB)

Two Brown Owls

Contents

Intro

Firstly, they're not related, not that they know of anyway. They simply share the surname Brown, very common in Jamaica. Jaqi's parents, were both Jamaican, as was Diana's father...her mother Italian.

They found it strange they hadn't met before, considering their many similarities. Both live in North Kensington, aka Da Grove/Portobello Rd, home to Notting Hill Carnival and are over 55 (that's as much as they'll reveal). Significantly, they were both signed music artists during the early 1990s. They're into crafting and keen hobbyists, from photography to fashion accessories and also happen to be human parents to small dogs.

Given these coincidences, the Browns were inspired to work together after meeting at a writing workshop facilitated in their neighbourhood by theatre director, Yasmeen Arden, who provided the foreword for this book.

At the intersection of show business and life, these self-proclaimed wise owls are here to reclaim their space, this time as authors. Songwriters in another life, theirs is a passion remained undiminished. They've extinguished their imposter syndromes and agreed to put themselves out there once more with intention. They gave themselves permission to extol their vulnerabilities for the greater good and authenticity of this project. Naturally, they're nervous about it. However, performance poetry and reading are baked in skillsets neither of them will ever lose.

They found the whole process an expression of

well-being and healing. With Jaqi a Soho House fellowship member, productive weekly meets were held at Electric House, Portobello Road and White City House.

The Brown Owls hoot from their own special branch of short stories, flash memoir, testimonial prose and the experimental that shamelessly explores misogyny, womanhood, identity, their inner voice and other external musings — this time on their own terms.

Currently un-agented, Brown Owls is just a taster — a demo of what they're about, as they actively pursue a traditional route to publishing…watch this space.

Foreword

I'm so honoured that Jaqi and Diana met and connected at our Creative Writing Group for 40+ Women in our very special community centre in North Kensington.

The writing group started as a one off, but it was obvious from the very first session how important it is for women to have this sort of place and space. The power of us coming together and speaking our words together is so beautiful and this power so clear to see in this collection of works from Diana and Jaqi.

Their collaboration is what it is all about. Building each other, owning our value and strengthening ourselves through being together.

Both Jaqi and Diana are accomplished and brilliant at what they do and they write with heart, wit and truth. They each have a very unique style and voice. Their words, like all our writers, are precious gold and that can't help but shine out.

I can't wait to see how this collaboration will continue to grow.

Yasmeen Arden
She/Her
@yasmeenarden

Diana Brown (DB)

Diana Brown (She/Her) has a lifelong interest in music, fashion and clubbing. Not necessarily in that order, but it cemented her relationship with Barrie K Sharpe, who was about to lead her on a monumental, life changing journey. A few years after meeting at a West End club, Barrie asked her to join a band and 'Diana Brown & The Brothers' was born.

But the road to success was a complex one. 'The Brothers' split and found fame as The Brand New Heavies and The Young Disciples. Despite the setback, Barrie and Diana produced cover track *Yes It's You* (FFRR/1987), which inspired their own 'groundbeat' genre/sound. When their single *Masterplan* (FFRR/1991) was released from the duo's album *The Black, The White, The Yellow and The Brown (and Don't Forget The Redman)* it became an acid jazz/rare groove club classic.

A teenager of the 70s, Diana had a passion for vintage fashion and a flare for sourcing the authentic that encompassed her taste for original style, which later translated into singing or songwriting. It was with some encouragement from Barrie that she found her voice and confidence in her songwriting skills.

After some years in the music industry, a trip to Thailand inspired her to make leather bags. She indulged her zest for market places with the spectacle and colour the clothes and accessories presented there. Back in London, she started label Stradastreetfashion and designed purses, clutch bags, leather cuffs, facial and body oils – all made with love.

'I only do things that I love. Life is too short.'

Diana Brown has found her voice again after completing her manuscript, a speculative dystopian love story, *The Shift To Pandemonium*. The writing workshop with Yasmeen Arden helped elevate her potential as a writer. Joining forces at the workshop with felllow singer Jaqi has been key to her growth in the literary arena.

For more info go to: Linktr.ee/DianaEBrown

Jaqi Loye-Brown (JLB)

Jaqi Loye-Brown (She/Her) is an emerging author and spokenword poet, and MA Creative Writing (Birbeck, 2022).

Before entering the spokenword arena (WOMAD 2023) this lady had a veritable chequered musical past. Dropped from major record label, Siren/Virgin, 1990/91, Jaqi shuffled from session to session with the likes of PWL (Anticapella) to Creation Records, Positiva to Antler Subway; She was the 'unsung' vocalist under a veil of aliases: Chilli & The Groove-gangsters, Jacqui Jair or Jacqueline Jair etc.

Knowing when to make tracks she turned the tables to work in music management. She left her record company

Assistant role at Dome Records to launch short-lived Almighty A&R (Leee-O). Jaqi took a sabbatical from music to become *Jax* 'in telly' (mostly BBC) for 10 years.

Jaqi, who lives in west London, five minutes from Portobello Road and its vintage markets and its eclectic demographic, describes herself as "a megalomaniac", home-schooled in guerrilla tactic creativity — music, spoken word, all matters digital and social, pre-loved furniture, arts and crafts, all of which informs her writing style. Born in the Midlands, but London based since 1989, she explores identity at the intersection of her West Indian/ Jamaican heritage and her British working class values.

Jaqi's collection of spokenword and short stories, her *Dutty Sink Drama Anthology* (Portobello Novella/MT-Ink, 2021), a nod to the Kitchen Sink Drama film genre, is available on major online book retailers — https://Bit.ly/DuttySD

The current day job, social media content provider, platforms her proven deftness for word play.

For more info go to: Linktr.ee/JaqiLoyeBrown

Two Brown Owls In Practice

Improv

JLB: Two Brown Owls sat in a bar discussing their future, contemplating their past and how it might furnish the time ahead

DB: Conversations of past relationships seem to be the general topic

JLB: It always come back to love

DB: Love & Hate seems to pop up regularly – fleeting

JLB: The negativity works harder before injecting positivity which makes a difference into the self

DB: Self-healing promotes energy and wellbeing...

JLB: Every breath is a triumph of survival for which we must give gratitude

Music

JLB: Who are the people unmoved by music?

DB: People who are moved will always be dancing

JLB: The movement external uplifting of souls

DB: Dancing is a trance thing

JLB: A practice for most religions over millennia and I wish it for the everyman – every man and woman alike

DB: Even babies love to dance in their cots when they hear music

JLB: It's a womb thing, not everyone gets to sing

DB: The heartbeat is the rhythm that unites us

JLB: Who are the people who are unmoved by music?

Goddesses (DB)

I am a Goddess and I come from a planet far far away

From the stillness of my universe, my pleasure is to look down on a planet called Earth

It is a troubled planet I see, full of human beings, who do not know how to behave appropriately with the abundance of what Mother Earth has delivered

I address womankind as Goddesses

In their dreams, I show them signs, and symbols

I show them the four elements of their Planet Earth whilst they sleep

I show them their own human potential in every dream

It is in their interest to take heed

I have an enemy, an opposer Who also speaks to the Goddesses in their dreams

They try to confuse them, make them weak, show them wealth in abundance

Not Mother Earth's wealth, but manmade wealth

Keep them as slaves is their promise to the sword

I want my Goddesses to RISE

To listen to Mother Earth and love her dearly

There is danger on Planet Earth

You cannot believe anything you hear or see

You have to feel to survive

Live a pure and simple life I ask you Goddesses, because when you pass over, Mother of all Goddesses will judge you

That is her work. She has been doing it for eons.

She will look into your soul

If She sees her reflection in your soul, you will be lifted towards the heights of eternity and feel happiness and joy for eons

If She cannot see her reflection in your soul, you will be born again and brought back to your planet, to the human experience once again, which will eventually become hell

31.01.2023

Faint At The First Sight of BLERD (Black Nerd) (JLB)

All the chat about AI prompted
Research
Where are the BLERDS in white coats?
Alas the all-black in white coats team of scientists remains fictional, a dusty dystopian manuscript
Where menacing, mad, melanin scientists run through biotic data – unleash their biases on an unsuspecting world
The kind Sci-Fi seldom created on screen
Imagine that...just me then?

Would BLERDS, peruse their findings, deceive intention, reassure us there is such a thing as a generic human
Empathetic human beings

Is there space for race in the quest for man to recreate man, in his only homogenous image
Is this an assumption or a societal myth, the scientific community have yet to shift
Shouldn't academics learn human first
Shouldn't we make academics feel human?
By definition scientists: a breed apart, the accidental creatives innovated by logic —sans emotions — robotic.

Heads in books, theories, ideologies, often loners or

misfits, underscores their socially awkward glitches
Humanised robot 'tis the goal, sensory bonding evolved, 'human-like'
Ahh, mostly men then? Meh!
Feel human to the touch?
Feel like humans' need for touch
Feel like humans – touched
Feel like humans repelled by human touch
Feel like humans untouched

The emerging age of existential conscientiousness consumes us while
AI's functioning at indeterminable pace
First prompt, here goes
Will racism occur encased in robotic malfunctioning
Will race be consigned to outer space?
For whom does future rockets zoom?
Whether literal or cerebral, it's no longer purely academic

In a world where circuits intertwine with prejudice's sting, Robotic malfunctions ignite, a troubled song they sing. Will racism, a haunting specter, infiltrate their core, Or will compassion's light illuminate a future to explore?

As gears turn, questions arise. Shall race be confined, locked away, transcending earthly bars

In the depths of outer space, can humanity truly find a realm where prejudice dissipates, leaving only love behind

Robots may falter, systems err, but hope refuses to cease, for within the realms of progress, unity seeks its release. In the symphony of progress, may harmony rise and replace A future where prejudice is erased, transcending time and space.

Does the man who makes machine
Make robotics feel human biases
Make robotics bypass human biases
Makes robotics steal human biases
Makes robotics conceal human biases

Every new thing in the world, hailed to serve for the greater good
Destined for the preserve of the greater greed first
Greatness bestowed on ideas that still shackle humans, unfed, unwatered, war mongered here on this planet
They plan it - intentions that will wipe out the planet
Everything in it, the many to perish the few to escape to Mars innit?
Who knows, but must robots feel?
How does man programme humanity that has yet to be achieved organically
In recent history, urban dictionary listed, 'the struggle is real'
Let the BLERD shed light, amass and demystify the robotics field,
Lest, Project 'Feel', descend, predictive soulless, doomed to fail
AI enigma, renege to thesis
Old skool, google searched, faint at the first sight of BLERD
A Sis, renowned scientist, roboticist,
Dr. Ayanna MacCalla Howard, a BLERD she most definitely is. There is hope. Word.

25.09.2022
(04.08 am)

As Day Turns To Night (DB)

As day turns to night and night turns to day

I switch my mind on your love

No matter what they say

It's ok, it's you that I want, my body feels lock-tight on you boy

You can fly, fly! On you boy, you can fly, fly.

I wanna know do I turn you on, the way you do as day turns to night

I wanna know do I turn you on the way you do as day turns to night

Cos my love is only right, no matter what they say no matter what they do

My love is only right, no matter what they say, they can't take my love away no

The Heart Wants What It Beats (JLB)

The heart wants what it beats

Up-tempo hover crafting momentum to

it's downtempo defeat

Where feet meets the eye, tears ran

aground heavy is the head; the will of lead

Replay the said, toil and till the unsaid

Deploy the joy revive the vibes

Ignite the air that pumped, once. Twice. Stumped.

The chamber churns, rinse cycle, sojourn

It ought to, aorta summons linen fresh beginnings

Random 30 second pressure release hastily come

Relieve me pitifully, grant you me

The sound of 'I'm done' hum drum, but freed to see

the blue I went to sea

Sand in hand there is hope yet for

Four, three, two and…

Time (DB)

Tragically time passes like a flash of lightning

Where did yesterday go?

The seconds on the clock tick-tock past

I am confused, what am I to do?

Do I have time to think of my time

Or must I avoid at all costs

I wondered why people put their life stories, on Facebook/Instagram/Tik-Tok.

It's to recall their time, via pictures, comments, words and actions

Ok, I can go with that, but still, time vanishes, before my eyes

Who can I speak to about time?

What would they tell me?

Oh, I understand now,

Time is about growing older and wiser

But…not everyone gets to grow old right?

So, is time like Russian roulette?

That's what time is (Living)

When your time runs out you must (Die)

Strange, strange phenomena, I must say

This is my Time; I have to go with the flow.

End Fucking Quote
(JLB)

Open quote
Am alone in a dystopian world where my phone orders pizza
Amazon isn't only the lungs of the Earth, but that which perma-altered our culture
Entertainment at my fingertips
From dating apps to gaming clips
Go partying or watch it online from a sofa
Facetime across the other side of oceans I may never go to
The strides made in medicine
The struggles in the distrust of them
Cars with GPS; A-Z out of print
Am I alone? Not according to drones or data sweeps
Ping a pound or two instant banking
Space tourism on the horizon
Advancements supersede our will to slow down than super speeds, our modern history's shown
Hello precipice. How much more in the name of progress is left to go?
Are we there yet?

Yet.

Skin.

Is.

Still.

A.

Thing.

End fucking quote.

31.10.21 (22.40)

Value Of Life (DB)

Who knows anything?

Who is anyone?

What a strange existence

Pretend you're happy

Pretend you have it all

Pretend you've figured it all out

Yeah of course you have

Pretend it's ok

Oh, look the love of your life is flirting

Pretend it's alright

The love of your life is lying to you

Pretend it's ok

Your best friend has utterly insulted your intelligence

Pretend you can handle it

Your new boss seems ok

You found out he molested three of the office girls,

Pretend that's ok

A few weeks in your new office job

Your boss comes up behind you at the vending machine and put his hand up your skirt

Pretend that's normal. He's only a man after all

You're famous now, you've had a baby with a producer

Pretend it's fine

He says he still loves you, but is never home

Pretend that's ok

He has been seeing another

Pretend that's ok

Scream and shout and let it all out

But still pretend you can handle it

Be strong, be strong they all say

Stay strong, stay strong they all say

Pretend you can

Love And Fame, A Poem (JLB)

You know love and fame
Can't live in the same place
Going all guns blazing starry eyed
At a heady pace

Fall and love hard
Somehow someday find
Success has a price
for a heart gambled

Love and fame
Sourced from emotionally similar places
You can't stay, but daren't leave
Non-committal on a par with heartbreak

Fame often denied
Where love survived
Believe be enriched
Choose love, love, love

Love and fame
One leads

One follows
By twists of fate
Hope or hollow

Experiments In Voice
(JLB)

Voice. Given it space. Ensured it had a chance to be heard, seen, felt

Projected beyond, unto the universe it flew

Care not if, nor why earthly ears listen

Communication in all the dimensions, formats, experimental artforms

Breath is a grammar lesson

Known love through it, scribed, lived in song

Sonically manipulated prose off the page

Experiments in voice, a journey long

When outcry takes over, too much said

The pieces say peace found

Stay

Hi, How Are You? Cried Julia (DB)

Jesus, how long has it been? Said, Mary

How have you been keeping?

The two women hugged each other.

The last time I saw you, we were at Joanna's house taking crack cocaine that evening do you remember?

Said Mary

Yeah, I do. Replied Julia

That flat was freezing cold. I'll never forget that, do you remember?

Yeah, I do. Said Julia.

What are you doing now? You still teaching?

No, replied Julia.

Funnily enough I met a fella about 2 years ago, at NA. She recalled.

He said he knew you, your name came up, can't remember why.

What was his name? asked Mary.

Stanley, Stanley McFadden.

Stanley McFadden.

Mary's ears pricked up. That was the name of her greedy ex-husband.

Stanley Mc Fadden, does he have black hair with a greyish tint, 6'8 slim, green eyes?

Yeah, that's him.

Oh, do you still see him?

Yeah, he's at home. We've been living together for a while now.

We are still on the crack believe it or not,

Julia said quietly, I am a functioning crack addict.

I am also on methadone at the moment, the crack led us both onto heroin

Is he still working in the city?

No, he stopped that kind of life. The cocaine got to him, then the crack moved in, he lost everything, including his mind.

Mary thought to herself what a coincidence bumping into Julia, for her to tell her she's living with Stanley. Strange, life it is.

Her ex-husband Stanley was a hedge fund manager

when she married him.

She recalled he was greedy for money. He didn't want to put his mother in a nursing home when dementia called.

Fact was he abandoned his mother to die alone in her rather large house.

Mary would never forget the scenario when she begged him to put his mother, Monica, in that private nursing home. He fought with her; he told Mary to mind her own business.

What goes around comes around...

The Black Napkin: A Cautionary Tale (JLB)

The waiter handed a small parting gift to each of the female guests, Kara and Jorja, as they made their way to the exit. The attendant held open the lift doors in the skyscraper, home to one of the world's premiere restaurants. They chatted along the way, for a moment excited by their exquisitely designed little keepsakes, with fine goldleaf work on rich, poppy red leather.

'Sorry about tonight...it was really, awkward. At least we have chocolate!' Jorja tossed her long, blonde tresses nervously, pursing her botoxed upper lips into annoyance..

'Yeah, not my favourite evening. Are you going to the bar or going straight to bed?' Kara shimmied her upper body playfully under her black shift dress. Her dark eyes steered far off beyond the guys.

'Not tonight. My bed's calling,' Jorja yawned.

'I wonder what the maître d' is saying to the guys?'

'I think they're talking about the black napkin.'

'Oh, no. I just want to forget about it.'

'I heard the maître 'd say, 'madam is upset with me tonight?'

'Did he? I feel so guilty. We had such a good time last time, he's a nice fella. Maybe it's company policy, not personal.'

'Kara, I wouldn't care whether it was company policy or not. I wouldn't do it. I'm so sorry you have to put up with that sort of thing.'

'I mean, he gave everyone a white napkin except me.

I was the only black person there and I get the black napkin? It wasn't even starched.'

'I know. It looked like a floppy worn out rag. It's outrageous. I can't believe it,' Jorja added, tucking at the waistband of her short ice blue cocktail dress. 'When you asked him to change it, he brought out another rag worse than before. Weird, so weird.'

'It was weird. His expression. He just did not want to give me a white one from that tray. I mean, what's that about?

'I gave him the filthiest look. Boy, if I'd said anything. Huh?'

'Here they come. Let's ask them...'

'I feel awful. I don't wanna make a fuss. Sometimes fine dining ain't worth it.' Kara trembled under the air con.

'Cheer up...I fancy a nice single malt on the terrace. Will you be joining us?' Alan rubbed well fed hands together.

'We're not in the mood.' Jorja piped up, eyes beckoning towards Kara. 'Anyway did you find out what's with the black napkin, did he say?'

John was last to shuffle into the lift, a tight squeeze with his salt and pepper head faced down. He rolled his tongue inside his lower lip, barely able to look at Kara. He shook his head and gave the nod to the lift assistant. 'Honestly, Kara...you've upset the poor man. He gave you the black napkin because it's customary to give patrons in black clothing – a black napkin. It wasn't because you're black. White napkins leave starchy lint on darker clothes. You're the only one wearing black...you twat,' scathed John. 'Jorja's wearing blue..and Alan. Look, I'm in grey, see?' His observations redundant by the mirrored bronze glow cocoon of the elevator.

'Oh my God! No.' Kara's mouth ajar, silently widened as the doors narrowed. In the last slither, the wounded eyes of the maître d', under the cadent hiss of closure.

War (DB)

Young Girl: Why are you fighting this war?

Prime Minister: Because we want to protect our land

YG: Why are you fighting this battle?

PM: Because we want to protect our land

YG: Why are you fighting this war, your citizens are dying, men, women and children.

YG: This land doesn't belong to you, it belongs to Mother Nature.

PM: We are fighting a battle to keep our land.

YG: But land belongs to Mother Nature, human beings do not own the land.

YG: You are sacrificing the human lives for land that you do not own.

YG: You are physically and mentally destroying man, woman and children, including animals

YG: Why are you fighting this wretched battle?

PM: Because we want to protect our land.

YG: You are physically and mentally destroying man, woman and children including animals.

YG: Why are you fighting this war?

PM: To protect our land

YG: No one owns the land it belongs to Mother Nature

YG: Do you not understand this?

YG: Isn't it strange how Prime Ministers send their citizens to war but they themselves do not go.

YG: This war is not about land, is it? Tell the truth.

PM: We need to protect this land.

YG: There is no point continuing. You just do not have a clue about life. If you did you wouldn't allow this tragedy to continue.

YG: Your citizens are dying of hunger, cold, thirst. They are living underground, babies have no milk, no warmth, no fresh water. This is deprivation, what are you doing? Can you not understand suffering?
One day you will.

PM: We need to protect our land.

YG: A land you do not own.

Big Scrubs (DB)

'The amount of stray dogs in Central London parks lately is crazy. This job has taken me all over town recently. A couple of weeks ago, I saw three roaming around one park. Last week at another place, five. This week in total, at least six or seven. It's terrible. Something is happening.'

Concerned dog walker Gina was was deep in conversation with colleague, Susie.

'I recognised a few of them,' said Susie. 'But none that I've had out with me.'

'The dogs seem nervous. I couldn't coax them to come to me if I tried,' replied Gina.

'I heard a few have been knocked down on Scrubs Lane and Du Cane Road,' said Susie.

One morning around 7am, Gina thought she spotted Susie's own dog, Jack, running around The Scrubs, lost. Where was his owner?

'Oh, maybe it's not Jack,' she thought for a moment, as the dog made its way over, but Jack jumped on her... he knew her well.

'Where's your mummy?' asked Gina, as if she'd get a reply.

Gina phoned Susie straight away, thinking she might be in the park looking for him.

No answer. She tried repeatedly. It went to voicemail.

'Hi Susie. Jack is with me, I've got him on a lead. We'll wait for you. I'm just in the middle of the park with my four, you can't miss us.'

Twenty minutes later, still no call back from Susie. Gina wondered whether she'd lost her phone or had an accident. Ever hopeful for an update soon, she walked the dogs around the park a little longer.

Almost an hour later, Gina headed home but first stopped at Susie's house, opposite the park. She rang the bell and knocked on the door — no response. She tried calling again, and left yet another voice message.

'Hi Susie, I don't know whether you mislaid your phone, but I'm outside your house. When you get this message, please call me. I've got Jack. He's fine.'

Gina wrote a note on the back of an old flyer, and wedged it in the letter box.

I'VE GOT JACK! CALL ME...
GINA xx

*****

Twenty four hours later, after members of Susie's family raised the alarm, a police investigation began. A day later, the UK's media descended on The Scrubs. A specialist search team assisted local police — swathes of officers, some with dogs, swept the Scrubs looking for any clues possible to Susie's mysterious disappearance. With her usual pack of dogs, now joined each day by Jack, Gina looked on in dismay as more police and members of the media camped out at The Scrubs, increasing by the day, and into a second week. But no crucial evidence, no signs of a struggle and no significant DNA or blood samples found.

The park keeper and every member of his team were interviewed and naturally under suspicion. Other dog walkers and owners were quizzed. Footage from the CCTV at the petrol station across the road on Scrubs Lane was downloaded and scrutinised. Thousands of local residents were questioned in the door-to-door interviews. Junkies, thieves and any local person on the sex offenders register were also targeted. Even the traveller site at the top of Latimer Road was visited.

Susie's family took part in television appeals — one of

her uncles cruelly tried by social media trolls claiming he was responsible.

Gina found it disconcerting to see her friend Susie's face plastered over the newspaper stands or dominating the TV news headlines when she returned home.

When will they work out what happened to her? When will it stop?

And then it did...

The media pack found another big story to focus on and the police scaled down their operation. The Scrubs slowly retuned to normal...whatever that was going to look like now.

*****

Nine months later, Steven Johnson and his sister Alison left their family home in Old Oak Common Lane on the other side Big Scrubs, waving goodbye to their mother at the door, as they left for school.

Steven had pinched two cigarettes from his mum's packet before they left.

'Straight to school you two, no messing about in the park and being late, you hear?'

Front door slammed.

'Those kids...' she muttered.

'Let's go over the other side of Big Scrubs for a smoke,' said Steven.

'Great,' chuckled Alison.

They walked across to the other end, the Scrubs Lane side.

'Over here...in there,' said Alison. Tucked away in the bushes, there was a small tree stump they both sat on.

'Light it, then,' demanded Alison.

'Ali, look. I've got some skunk.'

Alison raised her eyebrows. 'Did you nick that from mum as well?'

'Yep, I found it in her other cigarette packet – should

think it's Simon's, right?.'

'Yeah, probably. Mum makes him smoke it in the garden.'

'How much did you take?'

'Just this much. Shall I roll it?'

'Will we be able to get to school after we've smoked that stuff?' worried Alison.

'Of course, silly, it's only a tiny bit. Just let me roll it.'

'You got skins?'

'Of course, they were in with the skunk.'

'Nice...'

Steven rolled an untidy spliff, which looked like it might fall apart any second.

'How can we smoke this shit. Look at the way you've rolled it.'

'Never mind,' laughed Steven. 'Just light it...'

'Someone's coming, hide it.'

'No one can see us, just keep quiet.'

The schoolkids cowered, but they could see the pathway clearly. It was a jogger, then another one, followed by a woman wearing large headphones.

They could see a road sweeper in a high-vis jacket, pushing a cart laden with brooms, very slowly.

'There you go, Steven. That's what you can do when you leave school. Sweep roads.'

'Fuck off, I want to work in the city and make millions.'

'Not if you keep smoking skunk you won't.'

As a woman with a dog walked into view, the pair struggled to suppress their giggles.

But they were as quickly absorbed with the colourful markings on his hand and forearm, which they could see as the sleeve of his donkey jacket rode up. The glint of a large bloodied knife attached to the broom inked over his tattoos when it plunged into the lady's lower back. Her lifeless body collapsed onto the cart, and within seconds she was inside it. The kids gasped as the road sweeper appeared to tie the ends of a plastic bag together inside the cart...and then strolled on like nothing happened. The victim's dog sprinted in the other direction.

Steven and his sister, mouths wide open and hearts racing, bent down against the bushes holding the breath. Steven, an asthma sufferer, began to hyperventilate.

'Not now, Steven, not now...deep breaths...' whispered Alison. 'We need to make a run for it.'

'No. No,' panicked Steven, composing himself tearfully. 'Just shut up, we have to see where he goes.'

Heads in their hands, they waited for what seemed like a lifetime, half hiding, half trying to peer from the bushes. They couldn't be sure which exit the road sweeper left from.

'Let's go now!' said Steven, grabbing his sister's hand as they leapt through the bushes and ran home at speed.

*****

Steven and Alison's witness statement was case--defining.

Originally from Newcastle, the murderer's name was Tomas Odin. He'd been working odd jobs in London for years, living in Hammersmith. He wasn't even a road sweeper, or in any way attached to the park's workforce, which is how he'd somehow slipped through the net. He bought his dust cart from a film props company in Gateshead.

The court heard how Odin targeted green spaces with poor CCTV coverage, parking up in deserted lanes in an old van, from which he'd wheel out his customised cart, and then seek out his latest victim. He was now being linked to the mysterious disappearance of number of other females in green spaces around the London area.

A police psychiatrist concluded Odin's history of substance abuse left him with voices in his head, urging him to 'kill, kill, kill.'

Jailed for life without parole, Odin lived a miserable existence in a high security prison. Constantly targeted by vigilante lags, keen to add his scalp to their list of honour victims, he was thrown into one of the industrial-sized tumble-dryer machines in the laundry room one morning by 'the Daddy' of his wing. The injuries sustained during the 45 minutes he spent clattering around inside that huge drum were probably enough to kill him. His mangled body was found dead in a prison refuge truck.

Conversations With Demo Gods (I'll Never Have Again, Thank Fuck) (JLB)

Track 1:

'I'm recording a new demo, ya know.'
'Oh, yes? Where?'
'At Roy Shock's studio...Do you know him? Used to be in Viceroy Vice? They had that hit *See You Coming*?
'Ah...man, loved that track. How's he doing? What's he up to now?'

Track 2:

'I've written a load of songs for my demo...'
'How many tracks you doing?'
'I've recorded two tracks so far. Think I'm gonna do four...'
'You're gonna need at least 10, mate...'
'I can't afford to get that many done...I'm getting some studio time from, Roy Shock, you know, the one from...'
See You Coming? Yeah, I know him. He's a tosser!'
'Wha'? Why d'ya say that?'
'Ahhh, he's a f'acking idiot...'

Track 3:

'So, who's gonna be there? Might bring my demos with me.'
'Polydor, Colombia, EMI, Warner, Virgin, MCA...all the

majors. All 'a dem.'
'Think, you can you get me a squeeze?'
'Nah…it's one of them business only showcases.'
'Are you sure it's at Riverside? I might just rock up anyway…'
'Yeah…why not? Come check me.'

Track 4:

'That's track four…rewind, you missed the beginning.'
'TDKs are rubbish…you should…argh…'
'Stop. Try it now…'
'Do you play keys?'
'No…I sing the chords though …'
'You should learn. Same guy produced this?'
'Yeah…oh…I'm a bit pitchy there…'
'Do you have singing lessons?'
'Used to…but this is just a guide vocal…hopefully get back in the studio to lay it down properly.'
'Yeah, yeah, yeah…come back when you've done it. I'd like to hear it. Also keep the intros short.'
'Yeah, but…I'd love to record them in a bigger studio. Can't you get me in?'

Track 5:

'What? Sing something now? Right here, on the spot?'
'Yeah, hahaha, acapella…let's see what you've got.'
'What shall I sing…I can sing one of my own tracks?'
'Nah, give me some Mary J. or Whitney.'
'I'm more of your pop, commercial singer, a soft soul voice like Janet Jackson, Minnie Riperton…'
'Ok. Sing something.'
'I don't know which one, can't remember the words to anything…I prefer to sing my own songs really…'

Track 6

'I'm into all kinds of music, soul, pop, rock, jazz, but I'm

mostly into funk and disco. Singers wise I love Anita Baker, Deniece Williams, Tina and Whitney obviously...Chaka... and oh, Mica Paris!'
'Whoa...Mica can blow! What's she doing these days?'
'I dunno, but she's my favourite UK artist, there's not many, is there...I like Caron Wheeler and Juliet Roberts from Working Week, though...and I really like Lovers Rock singers, like Janet Kay, Carol Thompson, Jean Adebambo.'
'Yeah...Nice. Wait, a sec, check this...just had this girl drop her demo in, she's da' bomb man...she's a definite signing...'ere, listen...'
'Hmmm...she wrote that herself?'
'Yeah. She plays keys and guitar. The whole package. Can you believe she's only 15?'

Track 7:

'Yeah, I was signed to a major...'
'You was? Who with?'
'One of Virgin's labels...'
'What did you release?'
'Nothing. It was a three single, one album deal. Nice advance, but the AVL marketing team rejected it.'
'Probably a tax write-off. These labels do it all the time.'
'So I hear. Wish somebody'd told me beforehand, this could happen.'
'Aww, what kind of stuff was it?'
'Dance music. Just me and the producer on keys...was the thing back then,'
'Who was he?'
'No one you've heard of...but we did collabs with...'
'Anyway, so what you up to now?'

Track 8:

'Flooded? Oh, that sounds awful?'
'Yeah, have had to get humidifiers in and everything. Fucking mess.'
'So, when do you think, you'll be back up and running?'

'It's looking like a few weeks – at least!'
'Oh, no...what will you do in the meantime?'
'Dunno, will figure something out...I've got to take out and re-patch everything. Sorry to blow you out like this. I'll check you when all the kit dries out.'
'Well...if there's nothing you can do?'

Track 9:

'A remix? Who for?'
'I can't say, but it's for an artist on EMI...'
'EMI? Bloody hell...Come on, who?'
'Seriously can't say, but we're locked off for the whole week. Looking to do a rough cut by Friday and a mix down after that.'
'But it's a remix? Don't you wanna come in on a co-write with me, do your own original tracks instead of remixes back to back?'
'Babe, that's two gran'dage...can't pass that up. Don't worry I'll ring you.'
'Hmmm. But are you going to just take remix money when you can do both? Sooner or later they'll get bored and move on to another producer. At least you'll have some songs...'
'Hear you. But hands tied 'til next week.'
'Can I do a rough guide vocal to learn the track?'
'Not this week babes.'

Track 10:

'I love it! Sounding wicked!'
'Yeah...it's not messing about! Heavy...'
'Shall I go back in and do some ad libs?'
'Nah...Listen, I've gotta finish up now. My next session coming in a minute.'
'What? I thought we had the whole evening?'
'Well...it's just come in...I can't put them off. But come back next time and we'll finish it.'
'Can you run me off a copy then?'

'Yes, come back and will do one for you next time...'
'Please. I've been here all day. Just want to hear something, y'know? Here, I've got a spare tape.'
'Alright give me. Look, don't go playing this out to anyone. I know how you singers get.'
'Promise. It's just for me. I just want to familiarise myself with the track.'

Track 10 Instrumental:

'Could you test play it back so I can hear what it's gonna sound like on my stereo.'
'Ok, not the whole track though. I've gotta get set up.'
'Erm...sounds different, where's the sub bass and where've the cow bells gone?'
'No... some sounds drop out on the cassette. It's all there.'
'No. It isn't. Listen? There...that's when the chords should drop out...it's still full.'
'Look, take this one for now. Don't play it to anybody. Laters, yeah.'

Track 11:

'I've got plenty more songs...on some other tapes.'
'Tell you what, bring them with you. I'm hank marvin? Wanna grab a quick bite?'
'Er, could do.'
'We can chat a bit more about what's happening at the label and what we're looking for?'
'Sure...'

Track 11 Instrumental:

'Nice car.'
'Jump in.'
'Where we going?'
'This place where Naomi and George Michael go...it's not far.'
'Really?'

'D'ya mind if I just pick something up from home first... it's on the way.'
'Can't it wait?'
'Honestly, I'll be two seconds.'
'It's nice around here.'
'Yes it is, isn't it? OK. This is me. Two secs.'
'Hmmm.'
'Actually...come inside for a bit...let's have a cheeky glass before we go.'
'No. Thanks, though. You're alright. I'll wait in the car.'

Acknowledgements

Diana Brown

To my friends who have loved and supported me over the years. Thank you all.

Jaqi Loye-Brown

Thanks Matt (MT Ink) for his support and belief in my writing.

To Soho House Fellowship and membership support: the space to create in and inspiring creative spaces to thrive in. Salute Electric House and White City House. Aided by the odd Picante de la Casa and Porn Star Martini.

Birkbeck UOL and all that supported me through mypost grad, especially Ailsa & Jenni. Thank you. Not forgetting Prue and Luma.

Yasmeen for the invaluable time to create from authenticity with the amazing women in her work-shop who have also inspired me to playwright.

A special thank you to Liv Torc, The Big Girls Village and everyody who made our poetry performance at WOMAD Festival 2023 possible and so special.

Printed in Great Britain
by Amazon

31872386R00030